W9-DEX-067

Rainy-day Music

Written by Judith Jensen Hyde
Illustrated by Jason Abbott

Children's Press®
A Division of Scholastic Inc.
New York • Toronto • London • Auckland • Sydney
Mexico City • New Delhi • Hong Kong
Danbury, Connecticut

For Tom and Katie, with love. For family and
friends who have been patient. And for the
Juvenile Writers of Kansas City.
—J.J.H.

For Mom
—J.A.

Reading Consultant
Eileen Robinson
Reading Specialist

Library of Congress Cataloging-in-Publication Data

Hyde, Judith Jensen, 1947-
  Rainy-day music / written by Judith Jensen Hyde ; illustrated by Jason Abbott.
    p. cm. — (A rookie reader)
  Summary: Dad enlivens a boring, rainy day by playing "ghost fiddle," a musical activity involving
water-filled glasses.
  ISBN 0-516-24983-5 (lib. bdg.)   0-516-24998-3 (pbk.)
  [1. Music—Fiction. 2. Rain and rainfall—Fiction. 3. Fathers—Fiction. 4. Stories in rhyme.] I. Abbott,
Jason, 1972- ill. II. Title. III. Series.
  PZ8.3.H974Rai 2006
  [E]—dc22
                                                    2005016130

CHILDREN'S PRESS, and A ROOKIE READER®, and associated logos are trademarks and/or
registered trademarks of Scholastic Library Publishing. SCHOLASTIC and associated logos are
trademarks and/or registered trademarks of Scholastic Inc.
1 2 3 4 5 6 7 8 9 10 R 15 14 13 12 11 10 09 08 07 06

"It's raining," I said.

"I have nothing to do."

5

"It's too wet for my bike.
It's too wet for the zoo."

"Come here," said my dad.
"I'll make music with you."

"Bring six of Mom's glasses.
Be careful. Go slow!"

"Fill each one with water.
Some high. Some low."

"Pour some out of that glass.
Fill this to the brim."

"Now dip your finger
and rub 'round the rim."

18

"It hums!" I exclaimed.
"It buzzes! It rings!"

19

"It sings like a bow across violin strings!"

"It's a glass harp,"
said Dad.

"It's a harmonica,"
I exclaimed.

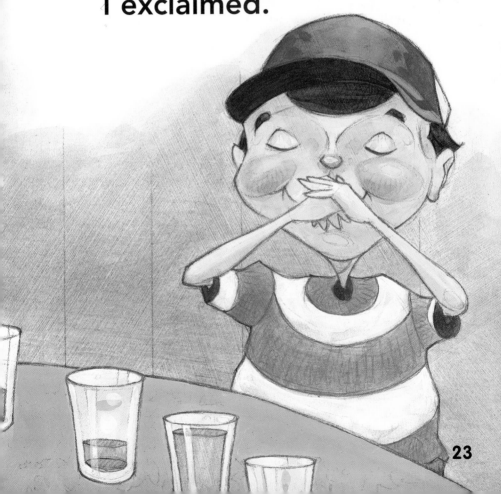

"Some call it a ghost fiddle. That's my favorite name."

Rain drums on our roof.
But now I'm glad!

'Cause I'm playing
ghost fiddle...

inside with my dad!

Word List (84 Words)

(Words in **bold** are story words that rhyme.)

a	drums	high	of	**slow**
across	each	hums	on	some
and	**exclaimed**	I	one	**strings**
be	favorite	I'll	our	that
bike	fiddle	I'm	out	that's
bow	fill	inside	playing	the
brim	finger	it	pour	this
bring	for	it's	rain	to
but	ghost	like	raining	too
buzzes	**glad**	**low**	**rim**	violin
call	glass	make	**rings**	water
careful	glasses	Mom's	roof	wet
'cause	go	music	'round	with
come	harmonica	my	rub	**you**
dad	harp	**name**	said	your
dip	have	nothing	sings	**zoo**
do	here	now	six	

About the Author

Judith Jensen Hyde lives with her husband in the Kansas City area. They have one grown daughter, one dog, and one cat. Every once in a while, after a holiday dinner, the whole family likes to play the ghost fiddle on Mom's best glasses.

About the Illustrator

Jason Abbott is a freelance illustrator who works in a variety of areas including magazines, books, and character development. He went to Savannah College of Art and Design and graduate school at Syracuse University. He lives in Atlanta, Georgia, with his wife and children.